Sherman's Adventures
Choices

Written and Illustrated by: Erin Birdsall

ISBN 978-1-936352-73-9
        1-936352-73-7

Published by Mirror Publishing
Milwaukee, WI 53214

Printed in the USA.

Erin Birdsall

Erin Birdsall has a passion for childrens and animals; especially cats! Erin grew up in Bay City, Michigan, and is a graduate of Bay City Western High School. Erin also holds an Associates Degree in Arts/Education from Delta College in Bay City, MI and later earned a BBA from Northwood University in Midland, MI. Erin currently is a social worker in the Cincinnati area, and resides in Northern Kentucky with her husband Bill and their two cats, Felix and Gabriella.

To Sherman:
You are missed every day.

And to Minxy and Blue:
May you find your way home

"Good morning class!" said Miss May, "We are going to do something different today!"

"Uh oh" said Felix, as he stood. "This could be bad or this could be good"

"Does anyone know what it means to make a choice?"

"I do," said Claudia, in a sweet soft voice.

"It means you decide what you are going to do. I make choices all the time and I bet you do too!"

"Very good Claudia!" said Miss. May. "You all make choices every single day."

"Let's start with this very easy question."

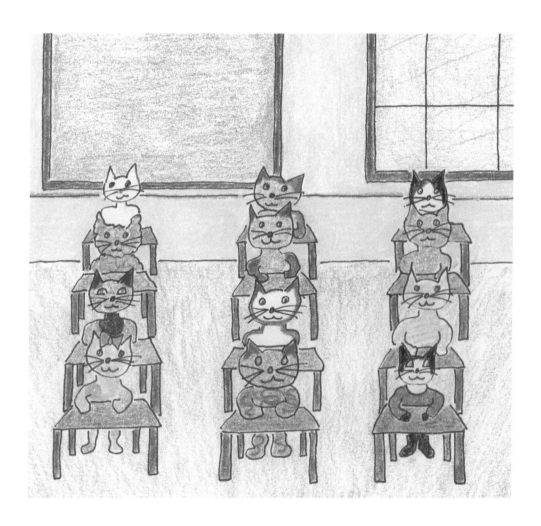

The entire class was now paying attention.

"For breakfast this morning, what did you eat?
Cereal, eggs or some kind of meat?"

"I forgot to eat breakfast today," Pie mumbled. And now her tummy rumbled and grumbled.

"I see," said Miss May. "Does anyone have something else to say?"

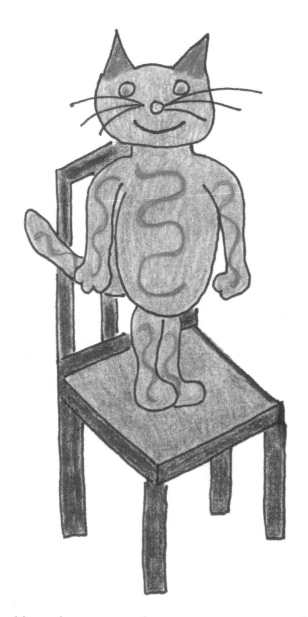

Again, Felix jumped up to stand. "Oops!" said Felix, "I think I forgot to raise my hand."

Miss May said to Felix, "That's okay....what is it that you wanted to say?"

"I ran up a tree when I was mad. That choice turned out to be really bad."

"I remember that day!" said Ella Sue, "a fire truck had to come rescue you!"

"I made a choice that turned out badly," said the new girl in class, a cat named Gabby.

"When I got really angry I used my paw, and punched my brother right in the jaw."

"That got me in trouble and in the corner I stood…
that choice turned out to be completely NO GOOD!"

Sherman now sat towards the back looking sick.
"Are you okay?" asked a cat named Rick.

"I chose to wear my bright green sweater, but I completely forgot to check the weather."

"Outside it looks to be getting quite hot," said Sherman's sister, the cat named Spot.

"I guess I should have done what I was told, but I really thought it was going to be cold!"

James then said "I must tell the truth."
I ate so much candy that I rotted a tooth!

"I now brush my teeth three times a day!

"I don't want more cavities, ICK! NO WAY!"

"Excellent examples," said Miss May, "but who has made a good choice today?"

"On Sherman's first day, he was shy, but I chose to be friendly," said the cat named Pie.

"And this morning when I was feeling really crabby…

…I chose to be happy," said the cat named Gabby.

"And the other day," said a cat named Jay…

"I got really mad. And I almost made a choice that was bad.

"I was about to yell and scream and sulk, but instead I decided to take a walk!"

Miss May then said with a very proud look, "I admire you all for the courage it took…

"To share so honestly, you should all feel proud!"
The class agreed and clapped really loud!

"Some choices are big, and some are small, but they all have a consequence, every one of them all."

"Every one, every day, has choices to make; it all depends on which option you take.

Who has control of what you do? Who you ask? The answer is you!"

The End

LaVergne, TN USA
29 August 2010
194951LV00002B